Hello,
Lulu

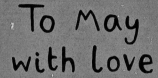

To May
with love

Copyright © 1999 by Caroline Uff

First published in the United States of America in 1999
by Walker Publishing Company, Inc.
First published in Great Britain in 1999
by Orchard Books, London

Library of Congress Cataloging-in-Publication Data
Uff, Caroline.
Hello, Lulu / Caroline Uff.
p. cm.
Summary: Simple text and illustrations introduce Lulu and her family,
Lulu's pets, best friend, and new shoes.
ISBN 0-8027-8712-6
[1. Family life--Fiction.] I. Title.
PZ7.U285Hg 1999
[E]--dc21   99-13813
                                         CIP

Printed in Singapore

2 4 6 8 10 9 7 5 3 1

Hello, Lulu

Caroline Uff

Walker and Company ✸ New York

This is Lulu.

Hello, Lulu.

This is Lulu's house.
"Come in!"
says Lulu.

This is Lulu's car.

Brrmm
Brrmm

This is Lulu's mommy,

and this is Lulu's daddy.

This is Lulu's baby brother.

He can say "lu-lu lu-lu."

This is Lulu's
sister.

She goes
to school.

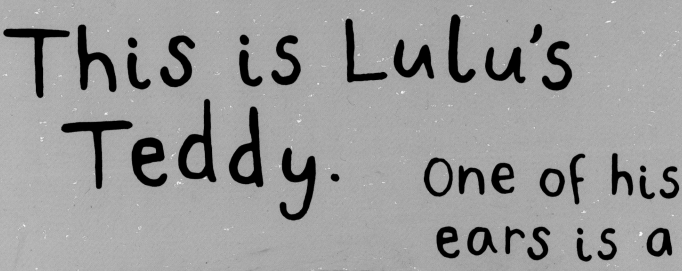

This is Lulu's Teddy. One of his ears is a bit wobbly.

Lulu kisses him
to make it better.

Look at Lulu's new shoes!

Red is Lulu's favorite color.

Lulu's family has three pets.

woof woof

snuffle snuffle

blub blub

Lulu's dog likes biscuits.

They blow beautiful bubbles.

pop!

This is Lulu's grandma.

Lulu likes snack time
at grandma's house.

But best of all,
Lulu loves her family,
and they all love her.

Bye-bye, Lulu!